Keira
the Movie Star
Fairy

For Jasmine Coppard, with love

Special thanks for Mandy Archer

ISBN 978-0-545-48496-1

Copyright © 2012 by Rainbow Magic Limited.

Previously published as *Keira the Film Star Fairy* by Orchard UK in 2012.

All rights reserved. Published by Scholastic Inc., 557 Broadway, New York, NY 10012, by arrangement with Rainbow Magic Limited.

12 11 10 9 8 7 6 5 4 3 2 1   13 14 15 16 17 18/0

Printed in the U.S.A.   40

First Scholastic printing, October 2013

Keira the Movie Star Fairy

by Daisy Meadows

SCHOLASTIC INC.

The Fairyland Palace

Meadow

Trailers

TEA · SNACK
REFRESHMENTS

Stepping-
Stones

Village

Jack Frost's
Ice Castle

The Woods

Gardens

Glade

Cottage

No more shall I lurk out of sight,
It's time I gave the world a fright!
Keira's magic things I'll steal,
To make a wicked movie reel.

If everything can't go my way,
Filmmakers shall rue the day!
A chill will fall on every scene,
Disaster for the silver screen.

**Find the hidden letters in the star shapes
throughout this book. Unscramble all 11 letters
to spell a special word!**

The Silver Script

Contents

Setting the Scene

"Look, there's Julianna Stewart!" whispered Kirsty Tate. "Isn't her fairy princess costume beautiful?"

Rachel Walker peeked around just as Julianna walked past. The movie star gave the girls a friendly wink, then sat down in a director's chair with her name on the back to study her script.

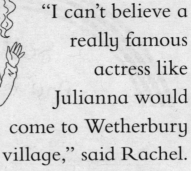

"I can't believe a really famous actress like Julianna would come to Wetherbury village," said Rachel.

"And I can't believe that she's spending most of our school vacation in Mrs. Croft's garden!" added Kirsty.

Mrs. Croft was a friend of Kirsty's parents, a sweet old lady who had lived in Wetherbury for years. Her little thatched cottage with pretty, blossoming trees in the front yard often caught the eyes of tourists and passersby. A few weeks ago when Mrs. Croft had been working in her garden, an executive from a big movie studio had pulled up outside. He wanted to use the cottage in

a brand-new movie starring the famous actress Julianna Stewart. When Mrs. Croft agreed, she became the talk of the village! Trucks full of set designers, lighting engineers, and prop-makers had turned up to transform her garden into a magical world. Now, filming on *The Starlight Chronicles* was about to begin.

"It was so nice of Mrs. Croft to let us spend some time on the set," said Rachel, watching the director talk through the next scene with his star.

Not only had Mrs. Croft arranged for the friends to watch the rehearsals, but when she'd heard that Rachel was coming to stay with Kirsty for a week, the kind old lady had also managed to get the girls parts as extras!

The pair had been cast as magical

fairies, helpers to Julianna's fairy princess in one of the most exciting scenes in the movie. It was the perfect part for them both — Kirsty and Rachel knew a lot about fairies! The two best friends had been secretly visiting Fairyland for a while. They never knew when one of the fairies would need their help, but they were always ready to protect their magical friends from Jack Frost and his troublesome goblins.

"I can't wait to try on our costumes," said Kirsty. "I wonder if they'll be as beautiful as real fairy clothes."

Rachel shook her head and smiled. All the sequins and glitter in the human world couldn't look as magical as a real fairy fluttering in her finery! Before she could answer her friend, the director tapped his clipboard with a pen.

"Attention, everybody," he called. "I'd like to run this scene from the top. We start filming first thing tomorrow and there's still lots of work to do."

Kirsty and Rachel exchanged excited looks as the set bustled with people. Helpers known as "runners" got props for the actors and showed the extras where to stand. Sound and lighting experts rigged up cables, while the dancers

practiced their steps. In this scene of *The Starlight Chronicles*, the fairy princess was due to greet the prince at a sparkling moonlit ball.

Kirsty and Rachel couldn't wait to hear the stars run through their lines! They watched as Julianna took her place

in front of Chad Stenning, the actor cast
as the fairy prince.

"And . . . action!" cried the director,
giving a thumbs-up.

Julianna coughed shyly, then stepped
forward.

"Your
Highness,"
she said,
making a
dainty curtsy.
"The air
shimmers
with enchantment
this evening. Shall we dance?"

Chad bowed. "Let the music wait a
while. Please walk with me on the
terrace. There is something I must say."

The crew watched, spellbound, as

Chad offered his arm to Julianna and led her off the set.

"Excellent work!" announced the director, making a note on his clipboard. "Let's take five."

Rachel and Kirsty chatted while the cast took a quick break. Runners rushed around the director, collecting notes and passing messages to the crew.

"I haven't seen that runner before,"
whispered Rachel, nudging her friend's
arm. "He seems to be in a big hurry."

Kirsty looked up as the runner elbowed
his way past the actors, then snatched a
script from the director's table. She tried
to see his face, but it was hidden under a
dark baseball cap. It was only when he
bumped her chair on the way out of the
garden that she spotted a glimpse of
green skin.

"That's no runner," Kirsty said
breathlessly. "It's a goblin!"

Right on Cue!

Rachel felt the back of her neck begin to tingle. If Jack Frost's goblins were in Wetherbury, it could mean nothing but trouble! She followed Kirsty's gaze and saw that, sure enough, two warty green feet were poking out of the bottom of the stranger's jeans.

"That's a goblin all right," she said. "We'd better follow him!"

Kirsty nodded and jumped to her feet, just as the director called "Action!" one more time. Before the girls could slip away, a group of actors rushed forward to act out a party scene in the enchanted garden.

"Good evening, Your Highness," piped up a girl in a fairy skirt. The man next to her elbowed the girl in the ribs and hissed, "That's *my* line, silly!"

The director rolled his eyes. "Take it from the top, please."

"Attention, fairies! Sinner is derved," babbled the man. "Oh, no! I mean 'dinner is served'! Or does that line come later? I can't remember!"

"Let's move on." The director frowned, turning to Chad and Julianna.

The cast and crew waited for the leading man and lady to start speaking. But instead of saying their lines, they stayed totally silent.

"Julianna?" called the director. "Julianna!"

Julianna looked helplessly at Chad.

"Is it m-me next?" she stuttered. "My mind's gone blank!"

The set fell into chaos as assistants scrambled to track down the correct page in the script.

"I don't understand," whispered Rachel. "Chad and Julianna have been perfect up until now. Something has gone terribly wrong."

"We have to find that goblin! I bet he has something to do with all of this," Kirsty said.

Rachel pointed to a path made of stepping-stones that curved around the back of Mrs. Croft's cottage. "He ran down there. Let's go!"

The girls hurried along the path, making their way into a pretty meadow behind the old cottage.

Normally the meadow was

a quiet place dotted with wildflowers, but today it was packed full of trailers in all shapes and sizes. The actors and crew had arranged to stay here while *The Starlight Chronicles* was in production. Kirsty and Rachel zigzagged around refreshment tents, equipment cases, and folding chairs, before spotting the goblin's baseball cap disappearing behind a fancy-looking silver trailer.

"That way!" cried Rachel, just as a rack of fancy fairy outfits trundled across their path. A costume designer with a tape measure around her neck smiled apologetically.

"Coming through!" she cried. "Sorry, girls."

Kirsty sighed. "We'll never catch the goblin now. It'll be too late by the time we get past these costumes."

"Don't be sad," said a voice as pretty as a tinkly bell.

As the girls tried to step around the rack, a cascade of tiny scarlet stars began to shimmer above the last dress in the row. It was the beautiful rhinestone-encrusted evening gown that Julianna was going to wear in the final scene. The stars began to sparkle and fizz even more brightly until a pretty fairy burst out of the dress and perched on the rack.

"Hi!" She smiled. "I'm Keira the Movie Star Fairy. You're just the friends I hoped to see today."

"Hello!" replied Kirsty

and Rachel, their cheeks flushing with excitement.

The fairy fluttered her tiny gossamer wings, motioning for the girls to follow her. As they dashed behind the next trailer, Keira's long scarlet gown swished in the breeze. It was made of the finest  fairy satin and decorated with glittering rhinestones. A gold starburst barette glittered in Keira's dark hair.

"It's my job to look after moviemakers

in Fairyland and the human world," she explained, when she was certain that no one else was nearby. "I've been watching over Julianna's career for a long time. She always shows such kindness to the animals she meets on location, so the fairies would like to say thank you.

I'm here to help make *The Starlight Chronicles* a big hit!" Kirsty and Rachel listened carefully as Keira went on to explain that she'd brought three magical objects with her from Fairyland. "The silver script makes sure that actors get their lines right every time.

The magical megaphone helps directors organize everyone on set, and the enchanted clapboard gets the cameras rolling. Everything was going beautifully until Jack Frost decided he wanted to be a movie star, too." She sighed.

The troubled fairy told the girls how Jack Frost had sent his goblins to Wetherbury. Their instructions were to snatch the silver script and bring it back to Jack Frost's Ice Castle!

"Julianna and the other actors won't be able to perform well without the script," said Keira, looking worried. "Will you help me get it back?"

Goblin
Glade

"Of course we'll help!" cried Rachel.
"We'd do anything for the fairies."

"We just saw one of Jack Frost's goblins
steal a script from the director's table,"
revealed Kirsty. "He ran behind that
shiny trailer up ahead."

"That must be my silver script!" Keira
gasped. "I bet he's trying to take it back
to the Ice Castle. Who knows what
mischief he'll cause by stealing it."

"If we run past those trailers, I'm sure we can catch him," said Rachel, leading the way.

Kirsty opened the top pocket of her jacket so that Keira could flutter inside.

"No one will see you in here," she said.

Keira peeked over the edge of Kirsty's pocket as the friends made their way

across the grassy meadow. When they got to the gate at the other side, the goblin had disappeared. The friends and Keira found themselves on the edge of a winding lane that led out of the village.

"I'll find out where the goblin went," said Keira. She waved her wand in the air. A haze of gold stars began to shimmer at its tip. The little fairy then moved her wand around to point in different directions. The stars got much brighter when it was pointing at the woods.

"This way!" cried the fairy.

Kirsty and Rachel ran to the edge of the woods, and peered through the trees.

"I can see the goblin." Rachel gasped,

pointing to a shady glade filled with ferns. "And he's not alone!"

There, in the dappled afternoon light, the goblin was pacing up and down with the silver script in his hand. He had thrown down his cap, revealing his long nose. He was holding his chin up as if making a grand speech. Behind him, a short goblin and one with very big ears were muttering together and shaking their heads.

"What's going on?" wondered Kirsty.

"When Jack Frost sends his goblins out to grab something, he usually wants them to bring it back right away."

"I think the goblins have decided to have some fun first," said Keira. "The one with the script looks like he's reading lines from it!"

"How funny! Who would have thought that goblins would like acting?" Rachel chuckled.

The girls crept slowly closer and crouched behind a raspberry bush so they could listen in.

"*I* have to be the director!" shouted the long-nosed goblin. "I'm the one who

found the silver script, and if you won't do as I say I'll tell Jack Frost what you're up to!"

"You can be the director if I can be the prince," snapped the big-eared goblin.

The short goblin kicked the tree next to him so hard the bump echoed around the glade. "That means I have to play the princess," he grumbled. "Yuck!"

The "director" laughed, and then pushed the goblin "prince" down onto one knee.

"Action!" he grunted, clapping his

hands together. As they shut, his fingers
knocked the prince's pointy nose.

"Ouch!"
snapped the
prince. "Will
thou marry
me, sweet
princess?"

Keira
fluttered
silently out
of Kirsty's pocket, coming to rest
on a branch.

"Oh, my!" she gasped. "They're acting
out the proposal scene from *The Starlight
Chronicles*. This is where Chad's character
asks Julianna to become his fairy bride.
It's supposed to be romantic."

"Go ahead," yelled the long-nosed

director goblin, pointing at the ugly
princess. "Pucker up for a kiss."

"Never!" thundered the goblin
princess.

"We have to follow the script!" the
goblin prince yelled. He snatched the
script out of the director's hands and
accidentally hit the princess on the head.

Within moments,
the goblins' secret
read-through had
turned into chaos.
The green trio
tugged and pulled
at the script,
shaking their fists
at one another.

The girls and Keira ducked back

behind the raspberry bush, trying hard not to giggle out loud.

"This little performance has given me an idea," whispered Rachel. "If it works, we should be able to trick the goblins into handing the silver script over to us."

"What's your plan?" asked Keira, her eyes shining with excitement.

As Rachel leaned in to share her idea with Keira and Kirsty, a twig caught on her sweater. It snapped with a loud *crack!*

"Who's there?" bellowed the goblin director, peering through the trees.

"Oh, no!" gasped Kirsty. "We've been caught!"

Putting on an Act

Rachel's heart began to thump. They were going to have to put her plan into action more quickly than she had thought!

"All we have to do is pretend that we know a lot about making movies," she whispered. "Keira, would you be able to cast a spell to give us some fancy clothes? We need to disguise ourselves as Hollywood talent scouts."

"Of course!" replied Keira, sprinkling a handful of fairy dust onto the girls. A fountain of golden sparkles shimmered over Kirsty and Rachel, transforming their outfits into grown-up business suits. They each felt a pair of dark sunglasses slip over their eyes.

"Now we look like real movie scouts!" exclaimed Rachel. "Thanks, Keira!"

Kirsty carefully opened her blazer pocket so that the fairy could hide again.

"Good thinking," said Keira. "If the goblins spot me, they'll realize that we've come for the silver script."

When Keira was safely hidden, Kirsty and Rachel popped up from behind the raspberry bush.

"Yoo-hoo! Over here!" they cried, waving their arms in the air to get the goblins' attention.

The goblin director peered through the

glade. When he saw the two girls, his
face broke into a terrible scowl.

"What are you looking at?" snapped
the goblin who was playing the prince.

Rachel stepped into the clearing.

"We were walking through this forest
scouting movie locations," she said. "We
heard your performance and thought
you might like a few tips. Your fairy
princess looks very pretty, but your fairy
prince is completely unbelievable!"

"Ha!" The goblin princess jeered at the prince.

"And what about you?" piped up Kirsty, pointing to the goblin director. "Surely you can get the actors to do better than that? I've never heard such confusing direction!"

The director snatched the silver script back from the big-eared goblin prince, clutching it closely to his chest.

"What do you know about movies?" he sniffed. "Have you seen a few on TV?"

The goblins all laughed. The director stuck out his tongue and waggled his fingers, while the other two blew noisy raspberries.

Rachel waited quietly until they calmed down.

"We're working on the movie that's filming in the village," she replied. "If you listen to our advice, I'm sure you three could put on a polished performance, too."

The long-nosed goblin director pouted and shrugged his shoulders.

"I guess we could use a little help," he admitted, "to uncover our star potential."

Rachel tried to hide her smile.

"Let's start with a few acting

exercises," she said. "I'll give you a scene to imagine, then you three have to act out what the characters might say. It's called improvising."

The goblin who had been playing the part of the fairy prince scratched his head.

"That sounds way too difficult," he said, sulking.

"Not if you think about it," encouraged Rachel. "Just try."

Kirsty held her breath. Goblins didn't like having to think too much.

"What about me?" complained the goblin director. "If the other two try this improvising thing, how am I supposed to boss them around?"

"You don't need a director when you're improvising," replied Rachel. "You can all try acting this time."

The goblin director glared at the goblin actors. Ordering them around had been his favorite part!

"Well," asked Rachel, "are you going to do it or not?"

A Perfect Performance

The goblin director paced up and down the glade, still clutching the silver script.

"Come on!" yelled the goblin who had been playing the fairy princess. "I want to give this a try!"

The goblin director screwed up his face.

"I don't want to!" he squawked, turning his back on the girls.

"That's too bad," sighed Rachel. "I was going to give you the starring role."

The goblin spun around. He was too vain to give up a starring role!

"I'll do it!" he cried, elbowing his two friends out of the way.

"Imagine that you're a great writer who just finished a really amazing new book," said Rachel. "Kirsty is going to play your publisher."

"Pretend you're coming to my office to deliver the story," Kirsty said.

The vain goblin puffed out his chest.

"That's easy!" he declared. "Just leave it to me."

The other two goblins scowled and looked like they were both about to complain. They didn't want to miss out on the limelight!

Rachel thought quickly.

"You two will play the writer's children," she decided. "Stay in the background for the moment."

"That's not fair!" shouted both goblins at the same time.

"Don't worry," said Rachel. "Your big scene comes next."

"Are we ready to start?" asked Kirsty. "Then . . . action!"

The long-nosed goblin swaggered across the glade, holding the silver script up in the air. "I'm here to see my publisher!" he announced, pretending to knock on an imaginary door. "My masterpiece is ready!"

The goblin tried to make his voice sound very grand and clever. Watching

through the trees, the other goblins forgot to be quiet and started to giggle.

"Please come in," replied Kirsty, playing along with the scene.

"I think you'll enjoy reading this," continued the goblin, handing her the silver script. "It's very special."

At that instant, Keira burst out of Kirsty's pocket. Quickly, the fairy swished through the air, a trail of golden stars fizzing behind her. She tapped the

silver script lightly with her wand,

magically
shrinking it
down to
fairy-size.

"It *is*
special!"
Keira laughed.
"Thank you for
giving it back,
Mr. Goblin Writer!"

It took the goblins a full five seconds to
figure out what had happened. When
they realized that they'd been tricked,
the threesome squawked with rage.

"Stop!" they shouted furiously. "That
script needs to be delivered to Jack
Frost!"

The goblins lunged and jumped for the

enchanted script, but Keira did a swift
loop-the-loop high in the air above
them.

"This is going back to Fairyland," she
told them. "Where it belongs."

"What are we going to do now?"
snapped the long-nosed goblin. "I'm not
telling Jack Frost."

"Me, neither!" howled the goblin with the big ears.

The long-nosed goblin scrambled into the woods. "Time to hide!" he wailed. When the silly goblins had finally disappeared, Keira smiled at Kirsty and Rachel.

"Thank you so much!" she exclaimed, magically changing the girls back into their normal clothes. "Now actors everywhere will be able to play their parts correctly. See you again soon!"

Keira tucked the silver script under her arm and vanished in a shimmer of fairy dust.

"Good-bye!" Rachel called after her. "It was nice to meet you."

Kirsty pointed the way toward Mrs. Croft's cottage.

"Let's go back to the movie set," she suggested. "I'll bet those rehearsals are on track again!"

"I hope so," Rachel replied, "but we should keep an extra-special eye out for those goblins. Who knows what Jack Frost will do when he finds out Keira has the silver script back. He won't give up that easily."

Kirsty nodded, linking arms with Rachel. Whatever happened, the girls would be there to help their fairy friends!

The Magical Megaphone

Contents

A Cast in Chaos

"We're here just in time!" said Rachel, opening Mrs. Croft's back gate. "Now that Keira's got the silver script, the rehearsals can start again."

The girls could already hear the director's voice from across the garden. He was reading out a list of names through his megaphone. All the actors playing fairies and elves were asked to

gather under the blossoming trees.

"Everybody needs to be in costume, please," called the director. "The engagement party scene is going to be a full dress rehearsal."

"Let's hurry," exclaimed Kirsty. "I don't want to miss a thing!"

The friends scurried back along the stepping-stones that skirted Mrs. Croft's cottage. Actors dressed as elves rushed past them, buttoning up velvet jackets. The costume designer the girls had met earlier was busy helping fairy cast members slip on gauzy wings dotted with sequins. A prop person handed out sparkly wands.

"Let's sit over there," suggested Rachel, pointing to a wooden bench tucked away next to the garden pond.

Kirsty happily took her seat, admiring the fountain that bubbled in the middle of the pond, rainbow colors dancing in its spray. This was the perfect place to watch a magical fairy rehearsal!

"There's Julianna!" Kirsty whispered, pointing across the garden.

The movie's leading lady stepped out from underneath a tree covered in pink blossoms. Julianna had a robe over her costume and a silk scarf tied loosely around her hair. She was listening closely to the director's instructions for the next scene. Chad was standing by some roses, waiting for a makeup artist to powder his nose.

"At least we know Julianna and Chad won't forget their lines now," murmured Rachel, relieved that the silver script was out of goblin hands.

"We'll start filming under the trees," called the director through his megaphone, "then the fairy servants should follow the princess as she flutters over to the rose arch."

Kirsty and Rachel both watched in admiration. Julianna had slipped her robe off her shoulders, revealing a lovely lilac gown. The star untied her headscarf and handed it to her assistant. A  diamond tiara twinkled on top of her hair, which had been curled in pretty golden ringlets.

"She really does look like a fairy
princess!" whispered Rachel.

"Let's roll!" announced the director.

The cast and crew fell silent, waiting
for Julianna to say her first line. Instead,
the actress delicately lifted the hem of her
skirt and walked toward the rose arch.

"The royal celebrations are ready to
begin!" she cried, curtsying in front of
Chad. "All of my
ladies-in-waiting
should be in
attendance."

Chad looked
very confused—
he was still
having his
makeup done!

The director picked up his megaphone.

"Miss Stewart," he said gently, "you're too early! The lines with your fairy servants should take place under the tree. *Then* you move across to greet the prince at the rose arch."

"That's not what you said," she muttered, wrinkling her nose.

The director coughed politely and shook his head.

"Can we try again?" he called. "Everyone go back to the flowering tree."

Julianna took

her place back under the tree and then
began to recite her lines. But when she
turned to speak to her costars, her fairy
servants had vanished from sight.

"Ladies-in-waiting!" bellowed the
director. "Where are you?"

Three actresses
wearing peach
chiffon dresses
peeked out
from under
the rose arch.

"We're over
here," replied
one. "Just
where you
told us to be!"

"Now there's no room for me!" Chad
complained, marching toward the trees.

"I'm going to stand with Julianna."

The frustrated director shook his megaphone in the air.

"No, no, no!" he wailed. "That's not what I said!"

Kirsty and Rachel swapped concerned glances.

"Something's wrong," said Kirsty. "No one has a clue what they should be doing!"

The girls watched in dismay as the director tried to fix the mess. Every instruction he shouted through the megaphone seemed to make things

worse. After a few more minutes, even *he* seemed to have forgotten where he wanted his actors to stand!

The rehearsal was in chaos. Confused actors stormed back to their trailers, leaving the crew to argue over what to do next.

"This is awful!" declared Rachel. "What are we going to do?"

Suddenly, the fountain in front of the girls began to bubble higher, shooting up a spray of silvery water. There, rising on the crest of the cascade, was Keira! The fairy waved at Kirsty and Rachel, but her face looked pale with worry.

Keira motioned the girls over to the bushes at the back of the garden.

"Will you come with me to Fairyland?" She gasped. "We don't have much time!"

Seeing Pool Surprise

Keira explained that Queen Titania had made a special request for Kirsty and Rachel's help.

"Her Majesty will tell you everything when we get to Fairyland," urged Keira. "Will you come?"

"Of course!" cried both girls at once.

A whirl of fairy
magic spun
around the
friends,
surrounding
them in a
flurry of
golden stars.
Kirsty and
Rachel felt
themselves suddenly getting smaller and
smaller until they were transformed into
fairies, with shimmering wings on their
shoulders.

The friends joined hands, then flew
toward the fountain. Sunbeams danced
in the spray, dazzling the three with
rainbow lights. Kirsty and Rachel closed
their eyes.

When they opened them again, they were gliding above the emerald hills of Fairyland! The hills were dotted with the scarlet rooftops of toadstool houses, and every so often a fairy opened a window to wave hello.

Before they knew it, the glittering pink towers of Fairyland Palace came into view. The friends landed gently in front of a pair of hedges that were trimmed in the shape of peacocks.

Keira led the way through the hedges into a lovely walled garden. Little paths meandered up and down the lawns, lined with pretty shells and colorful flowers. In the middle, there was a pond filled with exquisite water lilies. Kirsty and Rachel recognized this as the magical Seeing Pool. Queen Titania was standing next to the pool, her arm held out in welcome. The girls rushed over and curtsied.

"Hello again, girls!" the queen said warmly.

"Your Majesty," said Rachel breathlessly. "We came as soon as we could."

"We're here to help in any way we can," added Kirsty.

The queen smiled at the girls, but her eyes looked troubled.

"Thank you," she said with a gracious nod. "I asked Keira to bring you here because  *The Starlight Chronicles* is in serious trouble."

Rachel and Kirsty swapped worried glances.

"What happened?" asked Rachel.

Queen Titania stepped toward the Seeing Pool and waved her magic wand. The trickling waters instantly stilled and cleared.

"Come closer," she said as the pool began to shine with magical light.

Kirsty, Rachel, and Keira gazed into the enchanted waters. A picture of Jack

Frost slowly formed on the surface. The Ice Lord's face was creased into an angry scowl.

"That's Mrs. Croft's garden!" Rachel gasped, noticing the blossoming trees behind him. "What's he doing there?"

"When his goblins didn't bring back the silver script, Jack Frost got tired of waiting for them," explained Keira. "He stormed all the way to Wetherbury to find out what was going on!"

"He must have his heart set on becoming a movie star," said Kirsty.

When the friends looked into the Seeing Pool again, it showed Jack Frost

snooping around the movie set. Kirsty and Rachel frowned as he picked up a megaphone hanging on the back of the director's chair. He peered left and right to make sure the coast was clear, then stuffed the megaphone underneath his jagged purple cloak, cackling in delight. The friends shuddered as they heard him boast about taking the loot back to his frosty home.

"He shouldn't take things that don't belong to him," said Kirsty as the picture faded into bubbles. "The director needs that megaphone to do his job!"

"It's not just *any* megaphone," added Keira. "Jack Frost snatched my *magical* megaphone. I'd loaned it to *The Starlight Chronicles* to make sure filming went well! But if it's locked away in his Ice Castle, the director won't be able to get everyone organized."

Rachel thought back to the disastrous rehearsal. No wonder everything had been going wrong! How were they going to get the magical megaphone back?

An Ear-splitting scene

"Would you be willing to go with
Keira to Jack Frost's Ice Castle?"
Queen Titania asked the girls. "The
magical megaphone must be found
and returned."

Kirsty and Rachel both nodded their
heads.

"Of course, Your Majesty," said Kirsty.

"Thank you so much," said the queen, lifting her wand once again. "The magical megaphone should be easy to find. Its sound can travel for miles."

Queen Titania pointed her wand up to the sky. Multicolored fairy dust sparkled and flashed all around the fairies.

When the fairy dust finally settled, the beautiful gardens had disappeared. Instead, Kirsty, Rachel, and Keira found themselves in a dark forest.

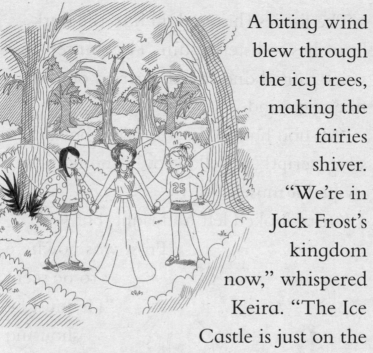

A biting wind blew through the icy trees, making the fairies shiver. "We're in Jack Frost's kingdom now," whispered Keira. "The Ice Castle is just on the other side of this forest."

Suddenly, a chilling voice echoed through the trees.

"You goblins are useless!" it cried.

"That sounds like Jack Frost!" Rachel gasped, looking nervously around her. "Where is he?"

The fairies fluttered up into the dark branches to listen again. The sinister voice ranted and raved, carried on the freezing wind.

"All you had to do was bring back the silver script!" it bellowed. "I should have swiped it myself!"

Kirsty looked left and right, but Jack Frost was nowhere to be seen. "He must be shouting through the magical megaphone!" guessed Keira. "Let's follow the noise."

Keira darted into the dark clouds swirling above the forest. Up there, the fairies could see jagged snow-capped mountains and the frosty-blue turrets of the Ice Castle jutting out from the surrounding gloom.

Rachel, Kirsty, and Keira flew straight toward the castle. As they got closer, Jack Frost's angry shouts boomed louder and louder.

"Watch out for the goblin guards!" said Rachel as the friends landed on the castle battlements.

Kirsty looked along the ramparts. At one end, she could see a pair of goblins on sentry duty, but they weren't paying attention. They were wobbling backward and forward, their  palms pressed to their ears. The fairies slipped past them, fluttering down to the castle courtyard. Down on the ground, the noise was almost unbearable. Kirsty ducked behind a pillar, then peeked back out.

Keira fluttered forward, but darted back the instant she spotted Jack Frost. He was pacing around the courtyard, shouting at his goblins.

"There are the goblins who stole the silver script," Keira murmured to her friends. "Jack Frost is yelling at them through the magical megaphone!"

The poor goblins were in a very sad state. As well as the troublesome ones

who had tried to steal the script, a mob
of other goblins had been summoned
from all over the castle. Some had their
fingers in their ears, others had ice packs
pressed against their foreheads. Jack
Frost's noisy shouting was giving the
goblins dreadful headaches, but he didn't
seem to care.

"Listen to me!" thundered Jack Frost at the top of his voice. "You need to start working on my first movie! I want you to steal some cameras and spotlights. I'm going to need a director's chair, too. . . ."

"We have to stop him," urged Kirsty, forced to shout over the din.

Rachel held her hands up to her head.

"But we can't get any closer," she cried. "The noise is deafening!"

Silence Is Golden

Kirsty and Rachel watched as the goblins tried to make sense of Jack Frost's ear-splitting demands. With their fingers in their ears, they were getting terribly confused. Some goblins bumped into one another and others wailed in protest at the horrible noise.

"We have to do something!" said Kirsty. "Jack Frost is sure to cause even more trouble now that he has the magical megaphone!"

"What was that?" called Rachel as the shouts got even louder. "I can't hear you!"

Kirsty frowned. It was impossible to hear a tiny fairy voice over this racket! Luckily, Keira knew just what to do.

She lightly tapped her wand against her ear, then whispered a spell to stop the horrible din:

"*Fairy magic, all around,*
Find a way to stop this sound!"

There was a flurry of golden stars as each of the friends suddenly felt a pair of earplugs slip into their ears.

Kirsty gave Keira a thumbs-up, enjoying the quiet. Even though they still couldn't hear one another, it was a relief to shut out Jack Frost's booming orders. She couldn't help thinking that the goblins would feel much better if they had earplugs, too. . . .

That's it! thought Kirsty. Keira had just given her a wonderful idea!

Keira watched Kirsty point to the

earplugs in her own ears and then gesture to the goblins. The clever fairy understood at once. If the goblins had earplugs, too, then they wouldn't be able to hear any of Jack Frost's schemes!

Keira gently tapped her ear with her wand once again, repeating the spell at the top of her voice. The wand sent a burst of golden stars streaming into the courtyard. The glittering stars flew over Jack Frost's head, but he was too busy ranting to look up. One by one, the stars landed on the goblins stumbling around the yard. As they touched the goblins' heads, a pair of earplugs slid into each one's ears. Soon every goblin in the castle was wearing a pair.

"Peace at last," one said, grinning.

"Can't hear a word now," boomed his crony. "Fantastic!"

Jack Frost chose that moment to hand out a job to each of the goblins. He pointed a bony finger at each one in turn. The goblins stared helplessly, not hearing a word he said.

"Get going!" he thundered, once he'd finished. "You all have lots to do!"

The goblins didn't move an inch. Instead of leaving, they just stared at their master. Jack Frost twisted his face into an angry scowl.

"*Get going!*" he repeated, bellowing even louder into the magical megaphone. "You heard me! Get on with it!" Keira, Kirsty, and Rachel shared a silent smile. They couldn't hear what Jack Frost was saying either, but they could tell their plan was starting to work!

The goblins began to mill aimlessly around the courtyard. Without clear

orders, they were useless! They saw that
Jack Frost was trying to say something,
but not one of them wanted to take their
earplugs out again.

Jack Frost's face turned purple with
rage.

"What's wrong with this thing?" he
snarled, shaking the megaphone and
peering inside it.

Rachel spotted her
chance. As quick as
a flash, she darted
inside the other
end of the magical
megaphone.

Jack Frost
narrowed his eyes,
trying to see what was
suddenly blocking his view. Rachel

wiggled up through the megaphone and
burst out of the other end, right into Jack
Frost's face!

"Argh!" he yelled, jumping back in
shock.

Keira zoomed out from behind the
pillar, rushing eagerly toward her
precious possession.

"That's mine!" she cried happily,
lifting the magical megaphone high into

the air. As soon as her hand touched the megaphone it shrank down to fairy-size.

Jack Frost howled with anger.

"Goblins!" he ordered. "Grab those fairies now!"

Back to Fairyland

Kirsty and Rachel followed Keira up into the air, being careful to fly out of Jack Frost's reach.

"Pesky fairies!" he fumed. "Come back here or I'll send my goblins after you!"

Jack Frost glared at his goblins, but they simply grunted, shrugged, and scratched their heads.

"They can't hear a word he's saying!" Keira chuckled, pulling her earplugs out. She motioned for Kirsty and Rachel to do the same. Once they had removed them, all three sets of plugs magically disappeared into thin air.

"What a worthless bunch!" barked Jack Frost, storming up and down the courtyard. "Can't you do *anything* I tell you?"

"What's up with him?" sniffed one of the goblins, nudging a pal in the ribs.

The other goblin couldn't hear his

friend, but laughed anyway. Jack Frost did look pretty silly stomping around the courtyard. "Time to go!" Keira beamed, pointing her wand at Kirsty and Rachel. The fairy's cheeks glowed with pleasure as a dazzling fizz of stars whisked the trio far away from the Ice Castle. The last things that Kirsty and Rachel heard were Jack Frost's shouts echoing in the distance.

"That was quick!" Rachel gasped, soon spotting the familiar pink towers of the Fairyland Palace shining up ahead.

"Look!" added Kirsty. "There's Queen Titania."

The friends landed gracefully in the palace garden, just beside the enchanted Seeing Pool.

"Welcome back!" said the queen, walking over to greet them.

Keira's eyes danced with pleasure as she held up the magical object for the queen to see.

"The magical megaphone is safe," the fairy said with a smile. "Thanks to Kirsty and Rachel."

Queen Titania held out her hands to the girls.

"I cannot thank you enough for your help," she said. "Now directors everywhere will be able to continue making movies for us all to enjoy."

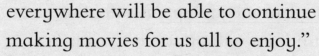

Kirsty and Rachel both curtsied, then turned around to share a hug with Keira.

Helping
Keira again
had been an
amazing adventure,
but it was time that
they went back to
Mrs. Croft's garden.
The best friends felt much happier
knowing that the dress rehearsal could
now go on without a hitch.

"Good-bye, Keira," said Rachel.
"We'll let you know how filming goes
on *The Starlight Chronicles*."

"Yes, please!" replied Keira. "Now that
the magical megaphone is safe, I'm sure
that Julianna will put on a sparkling
performance."

Kirsty told Keira and the queen about

an extra-special scene that they were
filming the next day. She and Rachel
were due to play their parts as extras in
the grand fairy wedding!

"Would you like to come and watch,
Keira?" asked Rachel.

Keira's face
flushed with
pleasure.

"Thank you,
girls!" she replied.
"I would love to
come!"

After everyone
said good-bye, Keira
hugged Kirsty and
Rachel. With a wave of her wand, she
turned them back to human-size and

sent them back home in a shower of
sparkles. The next time the friends met,
the girls would be in front of the
cameras!

"This vacation is going to be hard to

beat." Kirsty laughed as they arrived in Mrs. Croft's garden.

"It's about to get even more exciting," added Rachel. "Tomorrow we're going to be movie stars!"

The Enchanted
Clapboard

Contents

Camera Catastrophe

"Take your places, everyone!" called the director. "We're filming in five minutes."

Kirsty and Rachel were both feeling very excited. It was finally time for them to play their parts as extras in *The Starlight Chronicles*.

"I can't wait to show our costumes to Keira," whispered Kirsty, smoothing

down her frothy tulle skirt. Keira the Movie Star Fairy was due to arrive at any moment. After their adventure with the magical megaphone the day before, she had promised to come and watch them shooting their scene.

"You look just like a fairy helper," said Rachel, smiling at Kirsty.

"You, too," replied her best friend.

The girls had butterflies in their stomachs, but they couldn't wait to hear

the director say
"Action!" Soon
they would be
standing in
front of the
cameras with
Julianna Stewart, the film's beautiful
leading lady.

All the extras had spent a wonderful
morning in the hair-and-makeup
department. The wardrobe person had
dressed each girl in a pale pink gown
made of floaty material and embroidered
with tiny sparkling stones. Their hair
had been curled into tumbling ringlets
and topped with twinkling tiaras. Filmy
chiffon wings completed their
transformation into fairy helpers.

The first scene to be filmed was in the fairy princess's bedroom. The pretty set had been built inside Mrs. Croft's quaint old cottage. Kirsty, Rachel, and the other extras would be helping the fairy princess on the morning of her wedding.

"I hope I can remember where to stand!" said an extra named Angel.

Her friend Emily bent down to tie the ribbons on her satin slippers. "My hands are shaking with excitement!" she said breathlessly.

"Just do what I do," said a sweet voice.

"You're all going to be wonderful, I know it!"

Rachel and Kirsty spun around to see Julianna stepping onto the set. The star looked radiant in her flowing gown. Her skirts swished as she moved, making each shimmering layer catch 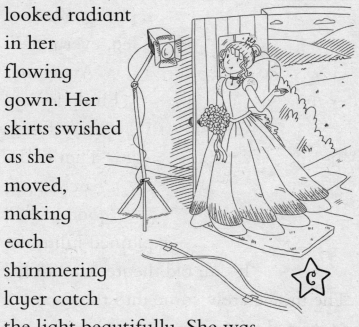 the light beautifully. She was carrying a bridal bouquet of peach-colored flowers from Mrs. Croft's garden.

"You look perfect!" exclaimed Rachel,

thinking about all the real fairies she had seen in Fairyland.

Julianna smiled happily at the girls. "Thank you," she replied. "Break a leg, everyone!" Angel and Emily looked confused. "That's how actors say 'good luck,'" explained Julianna. "It's an old theater tradition."

The movie crew came into the room and started to get the cameras ready.

Large, dazzling spotlights shone onto the sparkling set as the director held up his special movie clapboard. The

clapboard listed the name of the movie,
the name of the scene, and the number of
takes they'd done to get the scene right.
Kirsty and Rachel held their breath
with excitement.

"Here we go," the director said. "Quiet
on set, please. Lights, camera . . ."

The girls waited to hear the word *action*, but nothing happened.

"The clapboard is stuck," said the director, frowning.

The flustered crew tried to get the clapboard working again, but it refused to snap shut. An assistant ran up  and passed the director two thick wooden sticks.

"I found these in the props department," he explained.

The director grabbed the sticks and then called for everyone to be quiet.

"Lights, camera . . . ACTION!" He

knocked the sticks together to signal
everyone to start the scene.

Kirsty, Rachel, and the other extras
began to arrange the fairy princess's
dress, just as they had been told. The
girls tried very hard not to look into the
cameras that surrounded them.

"This is my last day as a fairy
princess," said Julianna. "Today I shall
become a—"

"Stop, please!" cried a voice, cutting Julianna's speech short.

"Who said that?" demanded the director. One of the camera operators waved his hand to get the director's attention. "My camera just . . . stopped," he stammered. "I don't understand." The director frowned, then held up the pieces of wood and clapped them together again.

"One more time, please," he called, after the camera had been fixed. "From the top."

"That means 'from the start,'" Julianna whispered to the girls.

She started to say her lines, but then there was a loud cry from the back of the room.

"Now my camera won't record!" exclaimed a second camera operator.

Another operator scratched her head. "Mine's the same!"

The exasperated director jumped down from his chair. Everyone on the set gathered around the cameras and started talking at once.

"Something funny is going on around here," whispered Rachel. "I can feel it!"

Keira's News

The director stomped out of the room in search of more cameras, and the rest of the movie crew trailed after him, chattering loudly. The other extras followed them, but Kirsty grabbed Rachel's arm.

"Wait," she said quietly. "Look—that camera's glowing!"

The friends stared as the shimmer spread around the camera lens. Then, in a flurry of golden stars, Keira whooshed out of the lens. The tiny fairy darted into the room and hovered in front of the girls. "I'm so glad you're here!" said Rachel excitedly.

But Keira didn't look happy at all. "Girls, something terrible has happened," she said. "While I was getting ready to come here, Jack Frost broke into my movie studio and stole my enchanted clapboard!"

Rachel and Kirsty were horrified.

"He was very angry when we took the

magical megaphone back," remembered Kirsty. "I bet this is his revenge!"

"What does the enchanted clapboard do?" asked Rachel.

"It makes sure that filming always goes the way it's supposed to," Keira explained. "Without it, even a big-budget blockbuster will end in disaster."

"That must be why filming is going wrong today," guessed Kirsty. "We haven't even been able to get through

one scene. Where could Jack Frost have hidden it?"

Keira looked even more worried than she had before.

"All we know is that he gave the enchanted clapboard to his goblins," she said.

Suddenly, there was a muffled, squawking giggle from outside the door, followed by the sound of footsteps on the stairs. The friends looked at one another in surprise.

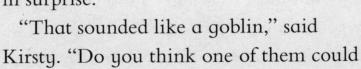

"That sounded like a goblin," said Kirsty. "Do you think one of them could

have brought the enchanted clapboard *here*?"

"It sounded like he was going upstairs," Rachel added. "Oh, no! There's another crew filming in Mrs. Croft's guest bedroom."

"We can't let him disturb any more filming," said Keira. "Come on!"

Keira darted under Rachel's ringlets, and then the girls ran out of the room and up the old wooden staircase. They were just in time to see a

green foot
disappear around
the top of the
landing.

"A goblin!
We have to
stop him,"
panted
Rachel,
reaching the
top of the stairs.

There were a couple of rooms with
half-open doors, but the goblin was
nowhere to be seen.

"Where did he go?" asked Kirsty. "We
have to find him!"

"We can't just walk into the rooms,"
said Rachel. "If the movie crew sees us,
they'll send us downstairs."

"Let me turn you into fairies," said Keira. "That will make it easier to look around without being seen."

"Good idea!" said Rachel.

Keira waved her wand and a cascade of golden fairy dust fizzed over the girls' heads. It twinkled in their hair and they shrank to fairy-size in the blink of an eye. Soon they were no taller than the cottage's baseboards. They fluttered the filmy wings that had appeared on their shoulders.

Rachel
zoomed
into the
air and
looped the
loop—it
was wonderful
to be a
fairy again!

Suddenly, they heard a muffled squeak
from behind the nearest door, which was
slightly ajar.

"I'd recognize that sound anywhere,"
said Kirsty. "Goblins! Come on!"

One by one, the three friends swooped
through the crack in the door into Mrs.
Croft's bedroom. Sure enough, two
goblins were bouncing up and down on
the bed as if it were a trampoline. One

was plump, and the other was skinny and had a warty nose.

Rachel clutched Kirsty's arm in excitement. The goblin with the warty nose had a large clapboard under his arm!

Goblin Hide-and-Seek

"That's my enchanted clapboard!" said Keira. "Oh, those naughty goblins!"

"It's my turn to play with it," the plump goblin complained in a loud whine. "You've had your turn. Jack Frost told us to bring it here and learn about making movies, and that's what I want to do!"

The skinny goblin did a somersault and clutched the enchanted clapboard even more tightly. "Why should you have it?" he said. "It's mine!"

"It doesn't belong to either of you!" declared Rachel, fluttering forward. "Give it back to Keira right now!"

"Fairies!" cried the skinny goblin.

He lost his balance and bounced off the bed with a loud crash.

"Shhh!" said the three friends together.

They didn't want the movie crew to come in and find the goblins! The skinny

goblin stood up, rubbing his head and scowling.

"That was your fault," he said. "Silly, pesky fairies!"

"Give me back my enchanted clapboard!" Keira demanded.

"No!" snapped the goblin.

He raced to the door, wrenched it open, and shot out at top speed. The plump goblin followed him, and Kirsty groaned.

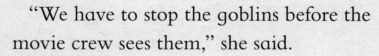

"We have to stop the goblins before the movie crew sees them," she said.

"And we have to get the enchanted clapboard back," Rachel added. "Otherwise the whole movie will be completely ruined!"

Keira, Rachel, and Kirsty zoomed out onto the landing. At the top of the stairs, the goblins were playing tug-of-war with the enchanted clapboard.

"Mine!" squawked the plump goblin, yanking the magical object toward him.

"Mine!" wailed the warty goblin, pulling just as hard.

Suddenly, the girls heard footsteps coming from behind one of the closed doors.

"What was that noise?" said a voice.

Rachel gasped. "Someone's coming!"

At that moment, the plump goblin lost his balance and both goblins tumbled right down the stairs.

The door opened and a blond woman peered out. Behind her, the girls could see a room full of flustered filmmakers. Two actors with red faces were scratching their heads, while the crew examined their cameras.

"I don't understand it," one of them said to himself. "Nothing seems to be wrong with it—but it just won't work!"

"I can't seem to remember my lines," muttered one of the actors.

The blond woman shook her head.

"What strange noises these old houses make," she said, closing the door again.

Rachel let out a sigh of relief.

"That was close!" said Kirsty.

"Come on!" Keira said, flying down the stairs after the goblins. "We have to keep them from causing any more trouble!"

Downstairs, the director and his crew were back on set, still

trying to make the cameras work. The
girls flew into the room and hovered
close to the ceiling, trying to spot the
goblins.

It was hard to see anything among all
the runners, extras, and actors. But then
Kirsty spotted one of Julianna's large,
frilly parasols. It was moving behind a
red velvet sofa in the corner of the room.
Four green feet poked out from
underneath it.

"There!" she cried, pointing.

As they flew lower, they saw that the goblins were still fighting over the enchanted clapboard. Just then, the skinny goblin used it to tweak the plump goblin's nose. He groaned in pain.

"Listen to those creaks," said a runner as he trailed a cable along the edge of the room. "Anyone would think this place was haunted."

"They're going to break the clapboard!" said Keira in an alarmed voice. "We have to stop them!"

Movie Mischief

"We can't do anything with the movie crew in the room," said Rachel. "We'll be spotted."

Keira peeked down at the movie crew. Actors, runners, and camera operators were calling out to one another and rushing backward and forward, trying to figure out what had gone wrong.

A sound technician had wedged her microphone in the old ceiling beams, and three runners were trying to pull it free. The wardrobe woman was in a panic because half her costumes had gone missing, and the makeup artist's brushes had fallen through the cracks between the floorboards. The poor director was sitting in the middle of it all with his head in his hands.

"This is the last day of filming on location," he groaned. "Mrs. Croft is coming back tomorrow. We have to get the wedding scene done by tonight."

The three friends stared at one another in alarm. They were running out of time!

"We can't stay here or we'll be spotted," said Kirsty. "Let's hide on the mantelpiece."

"Good idea," said Keira. "We can watch the goblins from there and wait for a chance to get the enchanted clapboard back."

They fluttered over to the fireplace.
They had just darted behind a pretty
porcelain figure when the director
jumped to his feet.

"Quiet!" he boomed.

That made even the goblins stop
fighting and stick their heads out from
behind the parasol.

"I cannot create movie magic in these conditions," the director went on. "Get everyone in here! Let's set up a screen and watch the dailies until the equipment can be fixed."

"What are dailies?" asked Rachel as the director's team sprang into action.

"They're the scenes that were filmed the day before," Keira explained. "The director always checks them to make sure nothing went wrong and needs to be re-shot."

The girls watched as two runners pointed a projector at the white wall above Mrs. Croft's sideboard. A production assistant carefully lifted a large reel of film out of a black leather case. The room was soon packed full of actors, runners, camera operators, and assistants.

"Let's make it dark in here," said the director.

A runner with a clipboard pulled the curtains shut and turned off the lights. Then the production assistant pressed

PLAY, and the scenes that had been filmed the day before were projected onto Mrs. Croft's white wall.

The room was dark and shadowy, but in the light from the dailies, Kirsty saw something moving behind the sofa.

"I think the goblins are trying to see what's going on," she whispered.

"Let's get closer," Rachel suggested.

Under cover of darkness, the girls swooped quickly down from the mantelpiece and fluttered closer to the goblins.

The goblins were watching the film scenes and scowling.

"Look at that silly fairy stuff!" said the plump one, folding his arms. "Who wants to watch movies about pesky fairies, anyway?"

"Jack Frost would make a much better movie," the skinny goblin agreed, tucking the enchanted clapboard under his arm. "And I would be the star!"

"No, *I* would be the star!" insisted the plump goblin.

"No, me!"

"*Me!*"

"Me!"

The skinny goblin jumped up on top of the sideboard, standing right in front of the projector screen. Everyone in the room gasped — it looked as if he had appeared in the middle of the movie scene!

"See how wonderful I look on-screen?" he demanded.

He struck a pose and put his hand on his hip . . . and the enchanted clapboard fell to the floor. The plump goblin made a dive for it.

"Quick — grab it from him!" cried Keira.

Fairy Movie Stars

Kirsty, Rachel, and Keira reached the enchanted clapboard a second too late. The plump goblin clutched it tightly to his chest.

"Give that back to Keira," whispered Rachel. "It doesn't belong to you."

"I'm not giving it to you!" the goblin squeaked.

The director frowned at the skinny goblin who had appeared in the middle of his scene.

"I certainly don't remember filming this," he said.

"Yes, and who's that ugly extra?" said Chad Stenning. "Who are you calling ugly?" squawked the goblin, blowing a noisy raspberry at the star. "I'm the best-looking goblin in the whole world!"

"Oh, no you're not!" snapped the plump goblin, jumping up beside him.

"Who hired these extras?" demanded the director. "And where did they get those hideous costumes?"

"They think the goblins are actors!" Rachel gasped.

The plump goblin gave the skinny one a hard shove. The outlines of their bodies filled the white wall behind them.

"I was born to be a star!" the skinny goblin yelled.

"No you weren't, *I* was!" the plump goblin squawked.

He flung the enchanted clapboard down on the carpet in a huff.

"Someone get those extras out of here!" roared the director.

"This is our chance!" said Rachel.

As a runner jumped up to remove the goblins from the room, the three friends zipped toward the enchanted clapboard. The crew was staring at the goblins, so no one saw the little fairy fly next to the enchanted clapboard and shrink it down to fairy-size with her touch. "I've got it!" she cried, lifting it up and then hugging it tightly to her chest. The runner was now chasing

the goblins around the room, and everyone was shouting and pointing.

"Come on," cried Kirsty, yelling over the din. "Let's fly out to the garden before the goblins realize that the enchanted clapboard is gone!"

They fluttered toward a gap in Mrs. Croft's curtains and swooped out through the open window. The afternoon sunbeams were dazzling compared to the dark cottage.

"We did it!" declared Keira.

The three friends shared a joyful hug.
Just then, they heard Mrs. Croft's front
door open. The goblins stomped out of
the cottage, scowling.

"I've had enough of moviemaking!"
the girls heard the plump goblin
complain. "I don't care what Jack Frost
says!"

The goblins disappeared into the
woods, and Keira smiled at Rachel
and Kirsty.

"Thank you for all your help today," she said. "Now filming can get back to normal. It's time for your scene!"

With a graceful swish of her magic wand, she returned Kirsty and Rachel to their normal size. Kirsty straightened her tiara, ready to go inside.

"Our big moment has arrived at last!" Rachel smiled.

"I'm going to take the enchanted clapboard back to Fairyland," explained Keira. "But I've got a feeling

that *The Starlight Chronicles* is going to be
a sparkling success. Break a leg!"

"Break a leg!"
called Kirsty
and Rachel,
waving
happily.

Keira twirled
her wand in a
tiny circle.
Then she
disappeared
in a burst of
golden light,
leaving behind
a shower of stars.

A runner popped his head out of Mrs.
Croft's cottage.

"Are you coming in, girls?" he called.

"The cameras are working again and we're ready for you."

Kirsty and Rachel hurried inside, their hearts fluttering with excitement. They arrived just in time to hear the director say some truly magical words.

"Lights! Camera! Action!"

Don't miss any of Rachel and Kirsty's
other fairy adventures!
Check out this magical sneak peek of

Autumn
the Falling Leaves Fairy!

Down on the Farm

"We could not have planned it better,"
Kirsty Tate told her best friend, Rachel
Walker, in the backseat of the Tates' car.
"It's the perfect weekend for you to visit.
The Fall Festival at New Growth Farm
is going to be so much fun!"

Rachel nodded and gave Kirsty a
bright smile. She could hardly get a word

in! Ever since she had arrived at Kirsty's house for the long weekend, her friend had been talking about the farm fundraiser.

"There will be apple picking, arts and crafts, and a giant leaf jump on the last day," Kirsty explained, too excited to sit still. She fiddled with her seat belt and swung her feet.

"Kirsty, dear," Mrs. Tate said from the front seat of the station wagon, "I'm looking forward to it, too, but please stop kicking my seat."

Rachel giggled. It was funny seeing Kirsty so wound up.

Kirsty decided to use her energy to tell Rachel more about the farm. "The best part is that my class has been going there on field trips," she said. "We feed the chickens, and help water and mulch the plants. We've learned a lot from Kyra, the farmer."

Rachel nodded again.

"I can't wait for you to see the orchards, and the rows of vegetables, and the duck pond. I know you'll love it all," Kirsty told her friend.

"It sounds like a magical place," Rachel said. She gave Kirsty a sly grin. After all, the two girls knew a lot about magic! They couldn't tell anyone, but Kirsty and Rachel were special helpers to Queen Titania and King Oberon, the rulers of Fairyland. The girls had worked with many of their fairy friends to outsmart Jack Frost and his tricky goblins. Most of all, they had kept the fairies a secret—if other humans found

out about Fairyland, fairy magic would
be in great danger.

"I'll tell you one thing we could have
planned better," Mrs. Tate said after a
moment. "The weather."

It was true. It was supposed to be a Fall
Festival, but it felt more like the peak of
summer! The sun was blazing hot. It was
a perfect day for swimming, but the pools
had been closed for two months! It seemed
like it was getting even hotter. The
weather forecasters couldn't explain it.

"You can't plan the weather, I guess,"
Rachel said with a laugh, but Mrs. Tate
just shook her head.

"I hope the heat won't keep people
away from the festival," Mrs. Tate
worried out loud. "Kyra's worked so hard
to make it perfect."

"Look! We're almost there," Kirsty called out. "Just around this bend."

But as the farm came into view, Kirsty gasped. All the plants in the field looked dry and wilted. As they drove by, the girls could see piles of rotten fruit on the ground.

"It doesn't look like I expected," Rachel said before she could stop herself.

"No," Kirsty agreed. "Something is terribly wrong." She looked out at the dry fields. The cows couldn't even find any grass to nibble on! She knew how much the weather affected farms, but Kyra's farm had been thriving a week ago. Now it was a mess. Something wasn't right.

"I can't believe I'm saying this," Kirsty whispered to her best friend, "but I hope

Jack Frost is up to his old tricks."

"Kirsty!" Rachel exclaimed in a hushed voice. "How could you hope that Jack Frost is causing trouble on the farm?"

"That's not exactly what I meant," Kirsty replied. "I just know something is wrong. I feel awful about what's happening here. But if it's Jack Frost's fault, we can do something about it."

Mrs. Tate was mumbling in the front seat. "It's probably this awful heat. Or maybe there are beetles attacking all the plants," she said to herself. She shook her head as she turned the car onto the farm's long dirt driveway.

Rachel thought about what Kirsty and her mom had said. If it was the weather or some kind of bug, there was no way

the girls could fix that. But if it was nasty
Jack Frost, Rachel and Kirsty knew just
what to do!

★   ★   ★

As soon as the engine stopped, Kirsty
hopped out of the car. "Come on,
Rachel!" she called. "Let's see how we
can help!"

Rachel was at her friend's side at once.
They could definitely help with the
farmyard chores, but they might be able
to do even more. "Let's look for signs of
Jack Frost and his no-good goblins," she
whispered. Kirsty smiled, happy they had
the same plan.

"Hey!" a voice called.

Rachel looked up to see a tall woman
in lace-up work boots taking long strides
toward them.

"You guys are real troopers, coming out in this heat," the woman said. She had a long blond braid down her back and crystal-blue eyes. "You must be Rachel."

Rachel returned her smile. "Yes. I'm visiting Kirsty for the festival. We're here to volunteer, if you need help getting ready."

"Yes, indeed," the farmer said. "I can't thank you enough. Suddenly, there's a ton of work to do around here. I'm not sure what's going on."

Rachel, Kirsty, and Mrs. Tate listened with concern. "Early this week, as the temperature got hotter, the fruit began to rot and the crops drooped," Kyra explained. "I can't seem to water them enough."

"Could it be some kind of bug?" Mrs. Tate asked.

Kirsty was wondering the same thing. She kept hearing a loud buzzing sound. She noticed that Rachel was looking around, too. Did she hear the same thing?

Just then, the buzzing became clearer. It was a whisper!

"Rachel, Kirsty! Look down!" the whisper said.

The girls locked eyes, then quickly dropped their gazes. They looked around the area near their feet.

There, hidden under the yellow petals of a squash blossom, was a tiny fairy! She was waving her arms up at the girls.

Kirsty quickly shifted her feet so that she was shielding the fairy from view.

When her mom gave her a funny look, Kirsty put on a grin and pretended to listen to the adults' conversation.

"Come over here and look at the corn," Kyra said to Mrs. Tate.

As soon as the adults were behind the tall cornstalks, Rachel and Kirsty kneeled down.

"Hello!" they both said.

"Hello, Rachel and Kirsty!" the fairy said as she stepped onto the blossom's stem. She was dressed in deep plum, golden yellow, and orange, with brown boots and long reddish-brown hair. She wiped teeny beads of sweat from her nose. "Excuse me," she said with a sigh.

"It's just too hot. I prefer cooler weather. I guess that makes sense, since I'm Autumn the Falling Leaves Fairy."

Kirsty and Rachel smiled. They loved meeting new fairies!

"The only problem is, unless you help me, there may not be any falling leaves this year," Autumn said, shaking her head. "In fact, there may not be any fall at all!"

"Oh, no!" Kirsty exclaimed. "No fall? Does it have anything to do with this strange heat wave?"

"It has everything to do with the heat," Autumn answered. "It's a long story, but it starts with Jack Frost."

Rachel and Kirsty weren't surprised. Jack Frost was *always* causing trouble! They listened closely to Autumn.

"I'm sure you know that Jack Frost loves winter. The freezing-cold weather fits his icy personality," Autumn explained. "This year, he couldn't wait for the cold weather, so he decided to try to trick nature and skip fall altogether."

"He wanted to go straight from summer to winter?" Kirsty asked, making sure she understood.

"Exactly," said Autumn. "And he knew just how to do it."

★   ★   ★

"What did Jack Frost do this time?" Rachel wondered out loud.

"He stole my three magical objects that get the fall season started," Autumn answered. "He was very clever. I didn't even realize that they were gone right away!" Autumn went on to list the three objects. She explained that the first, a scarf, brought the brisk breezes that were the first sign of fall. The second, a

pumpkin, made the fall harvest extra
magical.

The third object was a beautiful ruby-
red leaf. The leaf told the trees that it
was time for their leaves to change color
and fall to the ground.

Rachel looked around. The leaves were
still all green and on the trees.

"When summer was almost over,"
Autumn continued, "I went to get my
three objects out of their hiding place. I
always keep them in an old hatbox in
my closet. But this time, they were
gone!"

"If Jack Frost stole your objects," Kirsty
thought out loud, "why isn't it winter
now?"

"Because that's not the way nature
works," Autumn told the girls. "The

seasons follow a cycle. Summer leads to fall. Fall leads to winter, and so on. It isn't natural to skip a season." The fairy sighed again.

"So Jack Frost messed up the cycle," Rachel reasoned.

"Yes, and now we're stuck in summer until we can find my magical objects," explained Autumn. "The one good thing is that Jack Frost didn't want anyone to know he had the objects, so he hid them with a magical spell. I know that they are somewhere nearby. Now that I'm close, the goblins are trying to find them, too." She sighed. "If they get the objects, Jack Frost will hide them all over again."

"Not if we stop him!" Rachel said.

Kirsty put her hands on her hips.

"We've never let him win, and we're not going to start now."

Autumn nodded in agreement. "Then let's get to work," she declared. "But first, I have to take off this jacket! I'm so hot, I can barely think!" The fairy *was* wearing an awful lot of layers. Kirsty could tell she was too warm.

Autumn took off her jacket, and Kirsty tucked it into her pocket. "Let's hope you need this later," she said. Then the girls quickly asked Kyra for a chore that they could do around the farm.

"We're supposed to collect wood for a bonfire?" Rachel whispered to Kirsty after they had talked to the farmer. "It's hard to get excited about a bonfire in this heat."

RAINBOW magic™

There's Magic in Every Series!

The Rainbow Fairies
The Weather Fairies
The Jewel Fairies
The Pet Fairies
The Fun Day Fairies
The Petal Fairies
The Dance Fairies
The Music Fairies
The Sports Fairies
The Party Fairies
The Ocean Fairies
The Night Fairies
The Magical Animal Fairies
The Princess Fairies
The Superstar Fairies
The Fashion Fairies

Read them all!

■ SCHOLASTIC

HiT entertainment

scholastic.com
rainbowmagiconline.com

RMFAIRY8

RAINBOW magic™ SPECIAL EDITION

Three Books in Each One— More Rainbow Magic Fun!

Joy the Summer Vacation Fairy
Holly the Christmas Fairy
Kylie the Carnival Fairy
Stella the Star Fairy
Shannon the Ocean Fairy
Trixie the Halloween Fairy
Gabriella the Snow Kingdom Fairy
Juliet the Valentine Fairy
Mia the Bridesmaid Fairy
Flora the Dress-Up Fairy
Paige the Christmas Play Fairy
Emma the Easter Fairy
Cara the Camp Fairy
Destiny the Rock Star Fairy
Belle the Birthday Fairy
Olympia the Games Fairy
Selena the Sleepover Fairy
Cheryl the Christmas Tree Fairy
Florence the Friendship Fairy
Lindsay the Luck Fairy
Brianna the Tooth Fairy

■SCHOLASTIC

scholastic.com
rainbowmagiconline.com

HIT entertainment

RMSPECIAL11

RAINBOW magic

These activities are magical!
Play dress-up, send friendship notes, and much more!

📖 SCHOLASTIC

www.scholastic.com
www.rainbowmagiconline.com

HiT entertainment

RMACTIV3